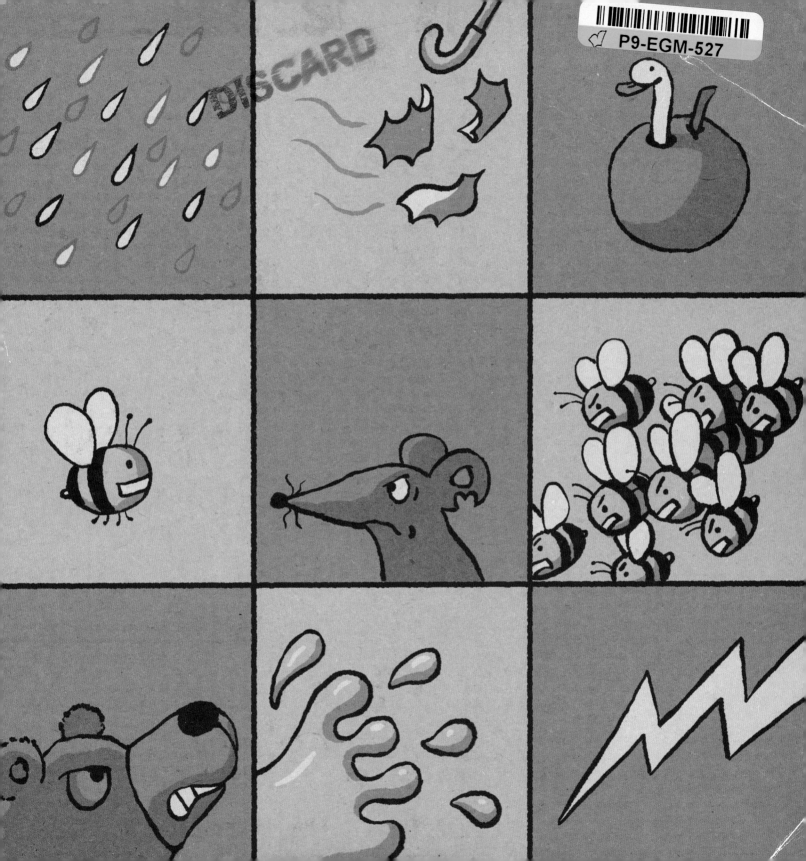

For Kellie

Library of Congress Cataloging-in-Publication Data

Mack, Jeff.
   Good news, bad news / by Jeff Mack.
      p. cm.
   Summary: While on a picnic, Bunny and Mouse see everything that
happens to them from opposite points of view—bunny sees only the
good, while mouse sees only the bad.
   ISBN 978-1-4521-0110-1 (alk. paper)
   1. Rabbits—Juvenile fiction. 2. Mice—Juvenile fiction. 3. Picnics—
Juvenile fiction. 4. Optimism—Juvenile fiction. 5. Pessimism—Juvenile
fiction. [1. Rabbits—Fiction. 2. Mice—Fiction. 3. Picnics—Fiction. 4.
Optimism—Fiction. 5. Pessimism—Fiction.] I. Title.

PZ7.M18973Go 2012
813.6—dc22
                                        2011016710

Book design by Sara Gillingham.
Typeset in Billy.
The illustrations in this book were rendered in mixed media.

Manufactured in China.

10 9 8 7 6 5 4 3 2 1

Chronicle Books LLC
680 Second Street, San Francisco, California 94107

www.chroniclekids.com

GOOD NEWS BAD NEWS

Jeff Mack

chronicle books · san francisco

Bad news.

Bad news.

Good news.

Bad news.

Bad news.

Good news.

Bad news.

Good news.

Bad news.

Bad news!

Very good news.